In those not so dim and distant days, before men milked their cows with milking machines, the fox had a piggy-like nose – in fact it was so piggy-like that it could almost have been called a snout. You would never have mistaken a fox for a pig however, as the fox did not grunt; it did not have trotters; it was covered with beautiful red fur and its tail was not curly, but long, bushy and called a "brush".

The foxes themselves were not worried by their flat, short, round, wet, ugly noses. In fact they thought they were beautiful. They could not imagine the elegant pointed noses that foxes possess today. You might find it strange that no pictures were painted of the fox's short, piggy-like nose. The answer is easy: they were simply not very good at painting in those not so dim and distant days.

But although the fox's nose looked strange and piggy-like before men milked their cows with milking machines, it was very useful. With his head held high, Reynard the fox could smell smells from near and far, high and low – strong smells and weak smells, delicious smells and disgusting smells. But from all the smells, near and far, high and low, strong and weak, delicious and disgusting, the one smell he liked best of all was the smell of dinner.

Now what did Reynard eat in those not so dim and distant days before men milked their cows with milking machines? His diet was simple but delicious. It consisted of slugs and bugs; voles and moles; cherries and berries; hares and pears; bees and peas; rats and bats and hens and wrens. In addition he had one very bad habit: he loved eating baby rabbit. So Reynard lived well; he liked his nose, he liked his dinner and he was happy. Then after he had eaten he slept and snored in contentment.

Occasionally, Reynard wou'
of his normal food of slugs and bugs,
voles and moles; cherries and berries;
hares and pears; bees and peas; rats
and bats and hens and wrens – and he
would even get bored with his terrible
habit of eating baby rabbit.

When that happened he would leave the
hedgerows, woods and fields and hold up
his nose to search for new smells – farmyard
smells. None of the new smells rhymed, but
they all made his mouth water. He could smell
ducks and geese; turkeys and bantams; eggs
and apples; marrows and plums; pig food,
hen food and the forerunner of Pedigree Chum.

Some days he could even smell the farmer's sandwiches. But the smell he liked best of all was the smell of cows. He did not eat cows of course – cows were too big – but he loved fresh, warm milk, cream, butter and cheese. No doubt if tubs of yoghurt had been invented in those not so dim and distant days he would have liked yoghurt too.

But how did he get at the fresh warm milk, the cream, the butter and the cheese? Today all the milk is in cold glass bottles or cartons; the cream is kept in refrigerators and the butter and cheese is sold in fancy boxes and wrappers. Even on the farms the foxes cannot get at the milk, for machines suck it out from the cows, and then it is carried along pipes to large steel tanks. From there it is sucked into great tanker lorries, to be taken to the dairy where it is bottled.

However, in those not so dim and distant days before modern men milked their cows with milking machines, the farmer milked his cows by hand, into a bucket. The cream was separated and put into another bucket, and cheese was made in the cool old dairy. So, when Reynard was tired of slugs and bugs; voles and moles; cherries and berries; hares and pears; bees and peas; rats and bats and hens and wrens – not forgetting the worst of his habits, chasing baby rabbits – he would try his luck in the farmyard, particularly in the cowshed and dairy.

If he wanted to creep up
extra quietly, he would put
foxgloves over his paws to
deaden all sound. After all,
that is how foxgloves got their name.
The farmer would milk the cows in the cowshed and
carry the milk and the cream into
the dairy next door.

As he carried it, some would always
spill out in those dim and distant
days and the fox's piggy-like nose
was ideal for finding it.

The farmer would milk twice
a day and he would do it by squeezing and
pulling the four large teats on the udder of
each cow, with his hands, two teats at a time,
and the milk would squirt, white, warm and
steaming, into the bucket. The farmer would squeeze
pull and rest, with a teat in each hand – squeeze, pull
and rest – squeeze, pull and rest. Each squeeze, pull
and rest took only about a second. To the cow it felt
rather like her calf sucking and so she would let her
milk flow.

Usually it would take about five minutes to milk each cow – 300 squeezes, pulls and rests – but the cows that gave a lot of milk would take longer and those that gave only a little milk would take shorter.

Sometimes when the farmer's hands were cold, or he was in a hurry, he would accidentally miss the bucket. He would squirt the milk in the wrong direction and hit his foot, his knee, or even spray the dog.

On those days, when the farmer was busy washing up his milking buckets in the dairy, the fox would creep into the cowshed and lick up all the spilt milk, before the cowshed was swept clean. Then, if the farmer was not looking, the crafty fox would try to lap some cream from the cream bucket or even nibble a bit of cheese.

It was by stealing cream that the fox got the white tip to its tail. One day the farmer's wife caught Reynard with his nose in the bucket. She was so angry that as she chased him she threw the cream at him, just catching the tip of his tail; that is why from that day onwards foxes had white tips to their tails.

Then a great change occurred: the not so dim and distant days, before men milked their cows with milking machines, suddenly became history as the electric milking machine was invented. It meant that instead of the farmer squatting on his stool to squeeze and pull the cow's teats, a machine did the same job.

Exhibits
A. Old milking stool
B. Ancient milk bucket

The four teat-cups would fit over the four long teats and then, driven by electricity, they would squeeze, suck and rest, squeeze, suck and rest. The milk would go from the udder, along a pipe and into a bucket that had a lid already attached, or into a large glass jar, high up from the ground. Each squeeze, suck and rest lasted about a second and the milk in the pipe went along in spurts. Feeling the pipe was rather like taking your pulse.

Ferdinand the fox was the young, well-mannered grandson of Reynard, and like his grandfather he sometimes became tired of eating slugs and bugs; voles and moles; cherries and berries; hares and pears; bees and peas; rats and bats and hens and wrens and, of course, his habit of eating baby rabbit. Then he would creep to the farmyard, and while Farmer John was in the dairy, washing up, he would tiptoe into the cowshed to lick up the spilt milk. But once the milking machine arrived he hardly ever found any spilt milk, or a bucket without a lid.

When Farmer John finished milking in the cowshed, he would switch off his machine by pushing a button in the dairy, before going into the yard to give his cows their hay. Then he would return to the dairy, switch on the machine to suck out the last few drops of milk from the pipes, before swilling down the cowshed with water, and washing the milking machines in a huge steaming sink.

Sometimes Ferdinand would tiptoe into the cowshed after the milking machine had been switched off and John, the farmer, was spreading hay in the yard for his cows. Occasionally he found small droplets of milk in the teat-cups themselves – as they hung on a post – but it was not like the old days and he never tasted cheese or cream. To get at the drops in the teat cups he would stand on his back legs, stretch up as far as he could stretch and lick them out with his long pink tongue. He would then stretch even taller and sniff each one with his piggy-like nose, smelling the warm fresh milk that had been sucked along the pipe and which he could never reach.

One day Ferdinand was feeling hungry.
He did not fancy slugs or bugs; voles or moles;
cherries or berries; hares or pears; bees or peas;
rats or bats nor hens or wrens, and he did not
even fancy his favourite bad habit of
scrumptious baby rabbit.

So he trotted off towards the farm.
Farmer John was in a hurry,
and as he hurried,
Ferdinand watched him
from underneath the
henhouse, hoping
to steal a quick
creamy lick.

John switched the milking machine on
from its button in the dairy and went into the
cowshed to milk the cows. One by one the cows
moved through and were milked, before
walking into the yard to wait for their hay.
Suddenly Ferdinand's heart leapt – silence –
the machine had been switched off and
Farmer John would be getting the hay.

Ferdinand crept into the cowshed, stood up on his hind legs as usual, stretched, and licked out the teat cups. The taste of milk was delicious.

Suddenly he heard a human voice in the distance: "Hurry up John – we will be late." It was Farmer John's wife calling to her husband.

Ferdinand was not worried as he could not understand English. John was worried, as he did not want to be late. It was his wife's birthday and they were going out to tea.

Ferdinand finished licking the teat-cups and stretched even higher to sniff each one, thinking of cream. John finished giving the cows their hay, and instead of approaching the cowshed as usual, he went straight into the dairy and pushed the button to start the milking machine, to suck out the last few drops of milk.

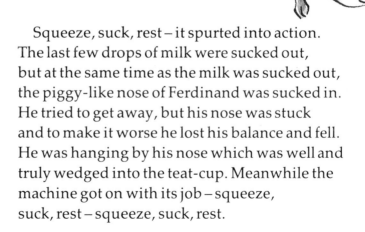

Squeeze, suck, rest – it spurted into action.
The last few drops of milk were sucked out,
but at the same time as the milk was sucked out,
the piggy-like nose of Ferdinand was sucked in.
He tried to get away, but his nose was stuck
and to make it worse he lost his balance and fell.
He was hanging by his nose which was well and
truly wedged into the teat-cup. Meanwhile the
machine got on with its job – squeeze,
suck, rest – squeeze, suck, rest.

Every time the machine went squeeze, his nose got narrower. Every time the machine went suck, his nose got longer, and every time the machine rested, he began to slide down towards the ground at great speed. But then, just as he was almost free of the machine, it would squeeze again, holding his nose like a vice. Then it sucked it up once more, before resting, when Ferdinand would begin to fall earthwards yet again.

SQUEEZE, SUCK, REST
– SQUEEZE, SUCK, REST
– SQUEEZE, SUCK, REST
– OUCH, UP, DOWN
– OUCH, UP, DOWN.
He could feel his nose
getting narrower and
longer and his eyes
watered. He wanted
to go home: it was like
being a living yo-yo.
SQUEEZE, UP, DOWN
– SQUEEZE, UP, DOWN
– OUCH, UP, DOWN
– OUCH, UP, DOWN.
Farmer John ran into the milking parlour
to wash it down and sweep it clean. He could
not believe his eyes: there was a fox with its
nose firmly stuck in a teat-cup, going up and
down like a yo-yo.
It was amazing.

He rushed into the dairy to switch off the electric motor. SQUEEZE, SUCK, REST – Ferdinand began to fall as he had done 299 times before. Suddenly the motor stopped and he kept falling, landing with a jolt in an enormous cowpat – the biggest cowpat he had ever seen, let alone sat in. He sat bolt upright, blinking and feeling his nose with his front paws.

Farmer John blinked too – a fox, sitting in a cowpat with a long, graceful, pointed nose, the first long, graceful fox's nose there had ever been. It was even more amazing than amazing.

Ferdinand got up and ran. He ran and ran, and as he ran Farmer John noticed that the white tip to his tail had disappeared because of the cowpat. So, from that not so dim and distant day until today, some foxes have had white tips to their tails and some have not. But, of course, since that not so dim and distant day too, all the foxes there have ever been have had long pointed noses.

Their new noses are even better for smelling than their old noses. There is another advantage as well: because of their smart new noses, foxes no longer snore. It is true – well have you ever heard one?